# RETURN TO TITANIC

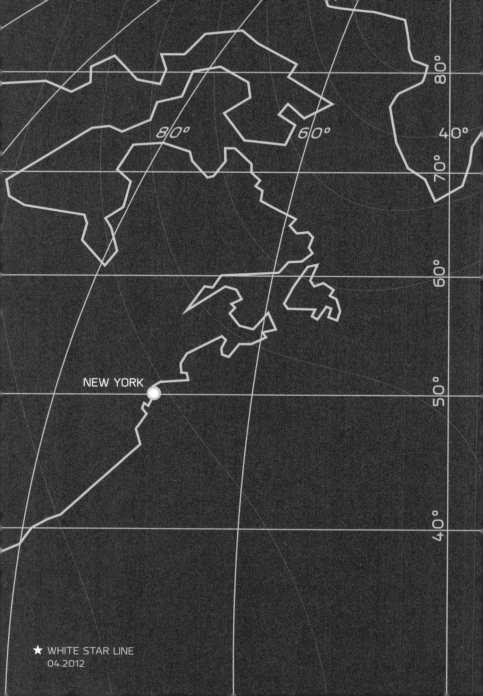

80°

60°

40°

80°

70°

60°

50°

40°

NEW YORK

★ WHITE STAR LINE
04.2012

by STEVE BREZENOFF

RETURN TO

# TITANIC

*STOWAWAYS*

2

ILLUSTRATED by SCOTT MURPHY

STONE ARCH BOOKS • A CAPSTONE IMPRINT

★ WHITE STAR LINE

SHIP **R.M.S. TITANIC** WEIGHT **46,000** [ TONS ]

DAY **10** MONTH **APRIL** YEAR **2012**

| | NAME | AGE |
|---|---|---|
| 1 | TUCKER PAULSON | 14 |
| 2 | MAYA CHO | 14 |
| 3 | | |
| 4 | | |
| 5 | | |
| 6 | | |
| 7 | | |
| 8 | | |

Published by Stone Arch Books – A Capstone Imprint • 1710 Roe Crest Drive, North Mankato, Minnesota 56003
www.capstonepub.com

Library of Congress Cataloging-in-Publication Data is available on the Library of Congress website.
Library binding: 978-1-4342-3300-4 • Paperback: 978-1-4342-3910-5

Summary: Maya and Tucker go back in time to convince *Titanic*'s captain to change the ship's course.

Image Credits: Courtesy of Mark Hodder, 78; Newscom: AFP, 110, Splash News, 111

Editor: Alison Deering
Designer and Art Director: Bob Lentz
Creative Director: Heather Kindseth

Printed in the United States of America in Stevens Point, Wisconsin.
102011 006404WZS12

# CONTENTS

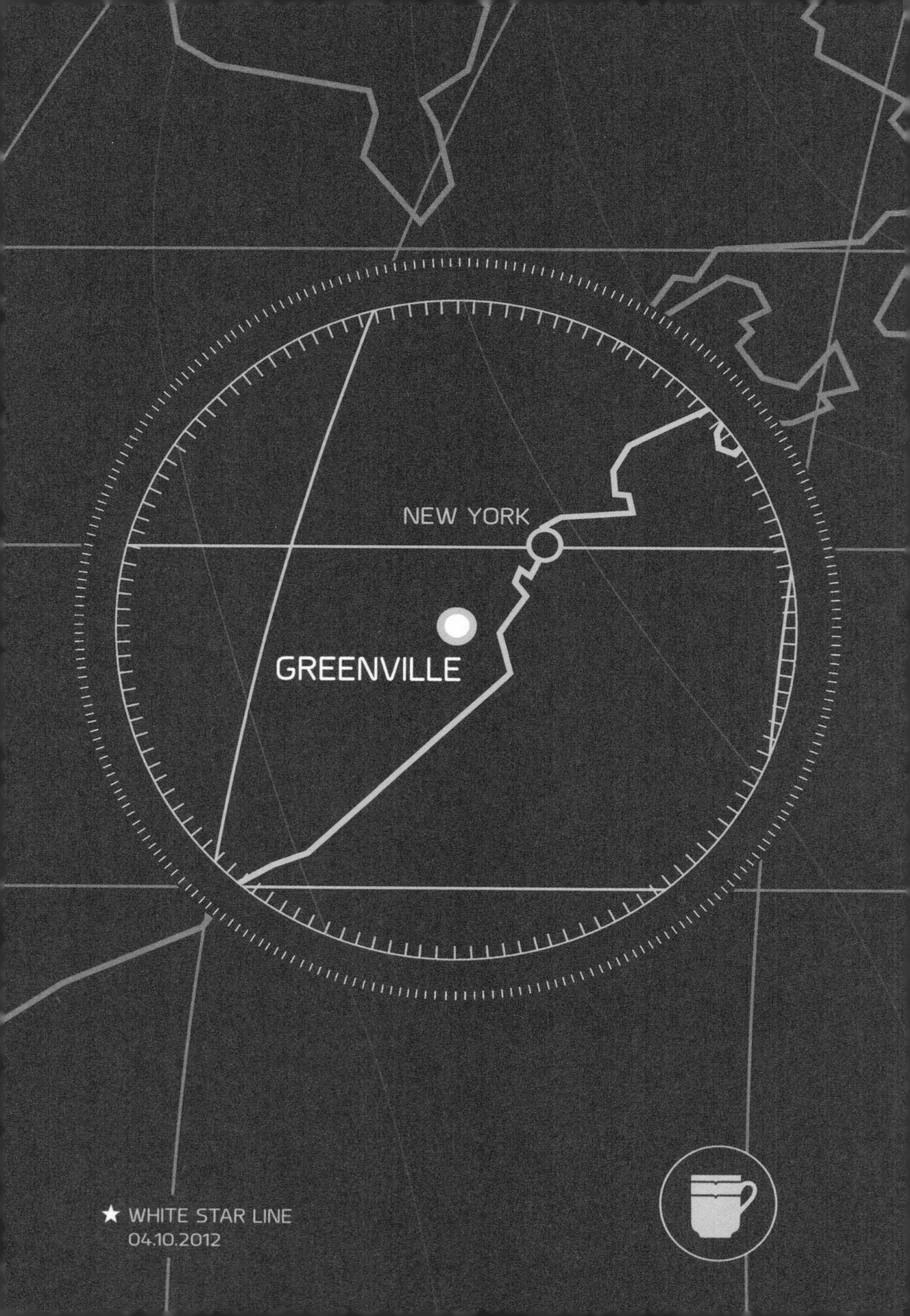

NEW YORK

GREENVILLE

★ WHITE STAR LINE
04.10.2012

# 1

# NO DAY AT THE BEACH

It was only the second day of spring break, and Tucker Paulsen was already exhausted. He let out a huge yawn as he sat on the front steps of the Greenville History Museum and waited for his best friend Maya Cho to arrive.

Tucker's mom had given him a hard time that morning about how tired he was when she woke him up. Tucker had made up an excuse about not going to bed early enough, and his mom hadn't questioned it. Thankfully. He couldn't exactly tell her the real reason he was so tired.

*I doubt it'd go over well if I told her Maya and I spent yesterday in Ireland*, Tucker thought. *In 1912.*

Tucker waved as Maya's mother pulled up in front of the museum. Maya hopped out and reached into the back seat to grab her bag. She waved as her mom drove away, then turned and hurried up the museum's big stone steps.

"You didn't have to wait outside for me," Maya said as she walked up. "I know how to get in."

Tucker nodded. "I know," he said quickly. "But I thought we should talk before we have to see my mom. You know, come up with a plan."

"A plan for what?" Maya asked. She strode up to the big double doors at the entrance to the museum and grabbed the handle.

"For how to get into the storeroom again," Tucker said. "Duh." He leaned against the door so Maya couldn't open it yet. "I hardly slept at all last night. I just couldn't stop thinking about Liam and his parents, stuck on the *Titanic*!"

Maya sighed. "Tucker, I told you yesterday, that happened a hundred years ago," she reminded him. "You worry too much. Now move."

Maya let out a yawn. Truthfully, she hadn't slept well either — and it hadn't helped that she'd stayed up late researching the *Titanic* online.

"We have to do something," Tucker insisted. "We have to figure out how to get back to 1912."

"I don't know if I want to go back, Tucker," Maya said, shaking her head. "Look, it's not that I don't want to help the Kearneys. I do. I just don't want to get stuck in 1912 forever. We're lucky to have made it back to the present once. I don't want to risk it again."

Tucker stared at her stubbornly. "We can't just give up," he insisted.

Maya sighed. "Any chance you're going to let this go anytime soon?" she asked.

Tucker shook his head.

"Fine," Maya said. "But let me handle your mom." She gave the door a strong jerk and yanked it open.

Maya marched in and across the main hall. She headed straight to Tucker's mother's office.

Tucker trailed a few steps behind her. "Wait!" he said. "Don't go in yet! We don't have a plan!"

Maya ignored him, "Hi, Mrs. Paulsen," she said, swinging open the office door.

"Oh, good morning, Maya," Mrs. Paulsen said. On her big wooden desk was a plaque that said Museum Curator.

"Tucker and I were wondering if we could be your assistant curators again today," Maya said. "We had so much fun yesterday." She smiled so her dimples would show.

Tucker noticed that Maya's voice sounded a lot sweeter than it had when she was talking to him on the front steps outside. Clearly she thought she could charm his mom into letting them back into the storeroom. Tucker rolled his eyes.

Mrs. Paulsen smiled at Maya in return. "Maya, I'm so glad you're interested," she said. "Tucker never expresses any interest in my work here at the museum." His mother looked at him pointedly.

"Uh . . . right," Tucker said. He tried to sound as interested as Maya. "Lots of fun."

His mother gave him a disapproving look. She wasn't falling for his act. "Follow me," Mrs. Paulsen said. She stood and picked up a very full keychain. "You two can work in the storeroom again. There's plenty back there that still needs to be cataloged."

Tucker and Maya followed a few feet behind Tucker's mom as she walked down the hall.

"I told you to let me handle it," Maya whispered to Tucker. "Your mom is a total pushover. No sweat at all."

Tucker's mom stopped at the door to the storeroom. She selected one of the keys off her heavy keychain, unlocked the door, and opened it for Maya and Tucker. Then she stepped aside.

"I'll be in the *Titanic* exhibit if you two need me," she said. "I'm expecting another big crowd."

"Thanks, Mrs. Paulsen," Maya said.

"Yeah," Tucker said, "thanks, Mom."

Tucker and Maya both walked in and headed straight to the box marked "Special Collection."

"Just be careful, you two," Mrs. Paulsen said. "Don't let me catch you taking anything out of its container, Tucker."

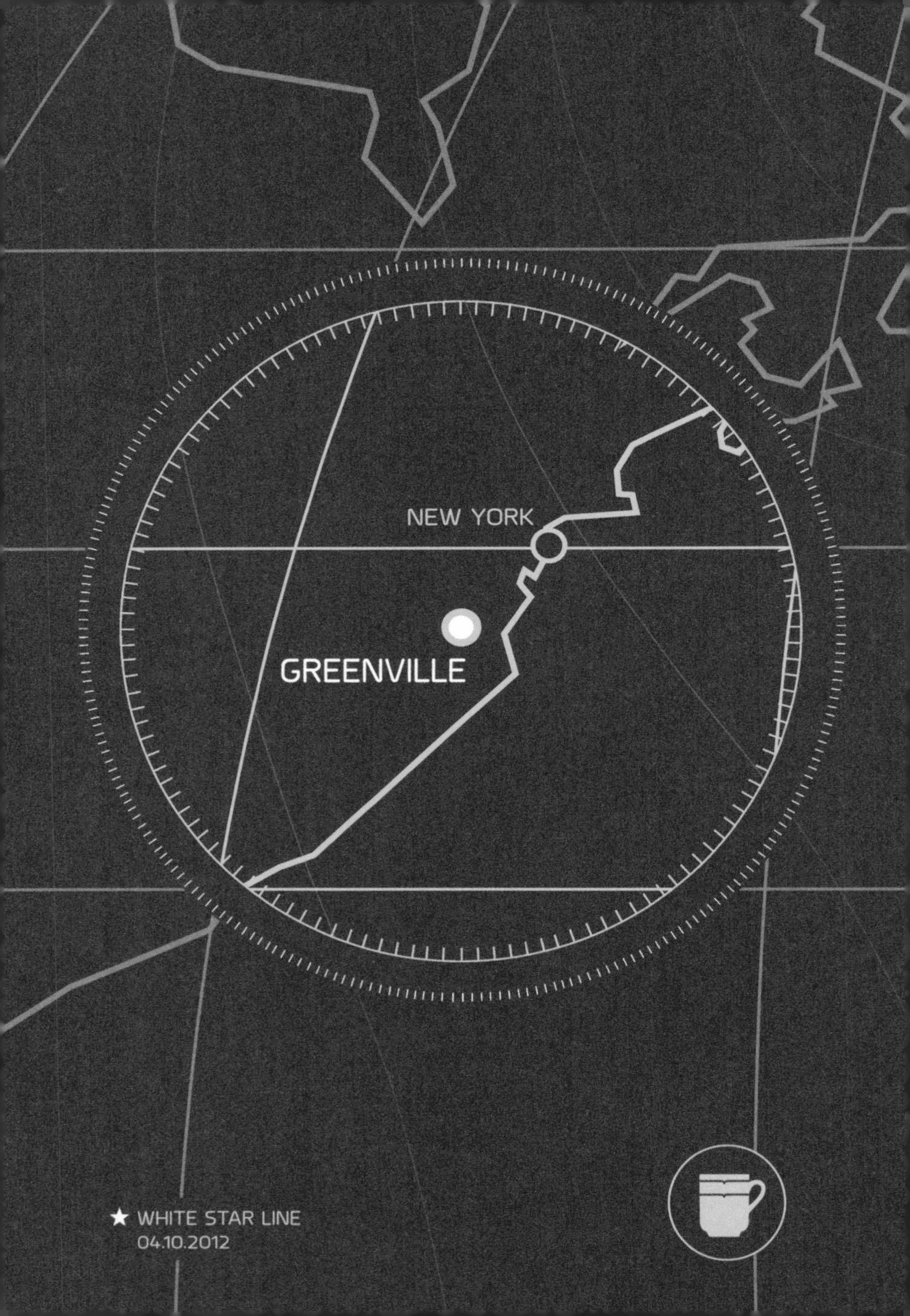

NEW YORK

GREENVILLE

★ WHITE STAR LINE
04.10.2012

# 2

# THE SPECIAL COLLECTION

"I'm pretty sure my mom likes you more than she likes me," Tucker said once his mom had left the storeroom. He sat down on the hard cement floor and leaned back against one of the metal shelving units.

Maya ignored him. "Okay, we're here," she said, looking around the storeroom. "But before we do anything, we have to talk about this. How do you know we're not going to get stuck in 1912 if we go back?"

"We know how to get back now," Tucker argued. "The second you want to leave, we'll leave. I promise. Okay?"

Maya sighed. "All right, fine," she said. "What's your brilliant plan?"

She reached over and opened the "Special Collection" crate. The same artifacts from the day before still sat inside: the boarding pass, a teacup, a smashed violin, and a life vest.

Maya poked at the old-fashioned life vest. It was yellowed with age and the straps were cut on both sides. She squeezed the vest inside its plastic wrapping. The canvas fabric of the vest was

ripped in several places, and underneath she could see what looked like cork.

"Well, we know the ticket won't work again," Tucker said. "We already tried it, and nothing happened."

"Maybe there's another ticket around here someplace," Maya suggested. She put the life vest back in the box and started looking at the boxes and crates on the shelves. "I mean, a ticket is used to travel, right?"

"Yeah, but I don't think it has to be a ticket," Tucker said. He scooted across the floor a few feet to look into the Special Collection crate. "I think it just has to come out of this box."

Maya headed back to the crate too. She pulled out the life vest she'd already looked at. "Okay, let's try this thing," she said. She was about to pull it out from the plastic wrapper.

"Wait!" Tucker said. He grabbed it from her and put it back in the box. "Not the life vest!"

"Why not?" Maya asked, sounding annoyed.

"Don't you see?" Tucker said. "That ticket we used the first time took us right to the dock in time for boarding. It brought us to the exact time we'd need a ticket."

"So?" Maya asked, shrugging her shoulders. "What's your point?"

Tucker dug around in the packing material. "So I think that life vest would probably take us to the exact time we'd need it," he said. "After the ship is already sinking!"

"And by then we might be too late to save Liam," Maya said, catching on.

Tucker nodded. "Exactly," he said.

"All right," Maya said. "Let's find something else to use, then. Something that will take us back to before *Titanic* sinks."

She joined him at the box, and together they pushed aside more packing material. Finally they uncovered the violin and the teacup.

"Which one do you think we should we try?" Maya asked.

Tucker looked
back and forth
between the violin
and teacup. The
violin was pretty
smashed up. Its
strings were all
broken and bent.
The neck wasn't
even connected to
the body.

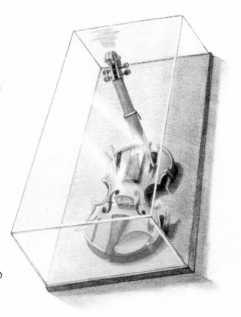

The teacup looked very fancy. Inside the solid
plastic case, the delicate cup was painted blue and
gold and white. Tucker picked up the teacup in
its case and studied it. It seemed to be in perfect
condition.

"The teacup," Tucker finally said. "I'm not
risking touching anything broken. This violin looks
like it's been through a war."

"Okay," Maya said. She reached over and took
the teacup from Tucker.

The plastic case didn't have a visible latch anywhere. "How do we get it out?" she asked.

Maya turned the case over and over in her hands, but she couldn't find a clasp. There didn't seem to be a way to open the case.

"We'll have to smash it," Tucker finally said. "I think my mom keeps a tool kit in her office. I'll go get a hammer."

"Smash it?!" Maya repeated. "Are you crazy? Your mom will kill us!"

"It won't matter," Tucker said. "Remember? Once we get back here, it will be fine. The ticket got ripped up yesterday, but when we got back, it was like we'd never even touched it."

"Oh, yeah," Maya said. "Okay, good thinking. Let's smash it."

"Wait here," he said. "I'll be right back."

Tucker walked to the door of the storage room and peered out. The hallway was empty in both directions. He quickly hurried toward his mom's office and slipped inside. Pulling the tool kit out of the closet, Tucker grabbed a hammer and hurried back into the storeroom.

Maya was waiting for him. She'd placed the teacup, still encased in plastic, in the center of the cement floor, as far from anything else as possible.

Tucker took a deep breath. He really hoped this worked. "Okay, here goes nothing," he said.

"Not too hard," Maya warned. "If you smash the cup, too, we'll be out of luck."

Tucker looked at her and nodded. "And in big, big trouble," he said.

He held the hammer close to the case. Then he lifted it just a little and brought it down lightly on the case. Nothing happened.

"Harder than that," Maya said. "Jeez."

"Okay, okay," Tucker said. "Better safe than sorry."

He tried again, a little harder. Still, nothing happened.

"Oh, for crying out loud," Maya said. "Give me that thing." She walked over and snatched the hammer out of Tucker's hand.

"Not too hard!" Tucker shouted.

Maya ignored him. She immediately lifted the hammer and brought it down on the case with a loud crack.

The case split into two pieces, and the teacup rattled across the floor for a few feet. Tucker

hurried over and picked it up. He breathed a sigh of relief. It seemed okay.

"You're lucky," he said. "That could have easily busted the cup."

Maya rolled her eyes. "But it didn't," she said. "So relax." She grabbed her messenger bag and slipped it over her head and across her body. Unlike the day before, this time the bag looked like it was stuffed full.

"What's in there?" Tucker said.

"This time, I'm going prepared," Maya said.

"What do you mean 'prepared'?" Tucker asked suspiciously. "What's in there?"

"None of your business," Maya said. "Are we going to do this or not?"

"We're doing it," Tucker said. He walked over to Maya with the cup and set it down on the floor between them.

"Ready?" Tucker asked. "We have to touch it at exactly the same time."

Maya nodded. "On three," she said.

Together, they counted out loud: "One, two, three!"

At the same time, Tucker and Maya grabbed the cup. And in a flash of light, they were gone.

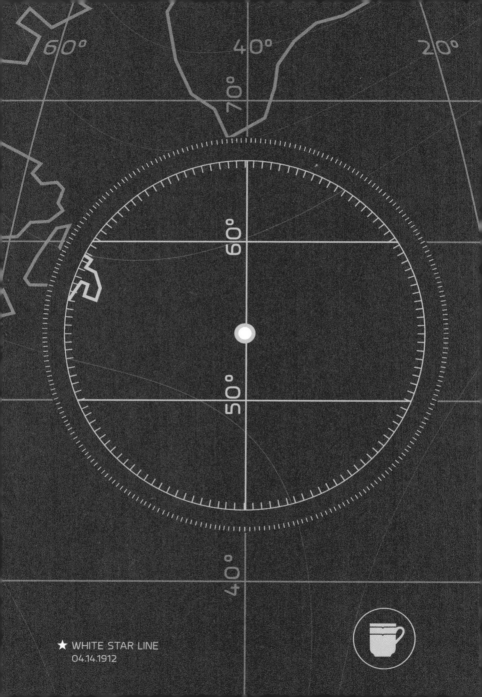

60°  40°  20°

70°

60°

50°

40°

★ WHITE STAR LINE
04.14.1912

# TRAPPED

Tucker put a hand to his head and groaned. His head was pounding. Time travel was not pleasant business, he was learning.

Maya poked him. "Wake up," she said.

"I'm awake," Tucker said. "Where are we?"

"You tell me," Maya said. "I don't think we're on a boat. It doesn't look like any boat I've ever seen, at least. Not that I've seen many."

Tucker squinted. Nearby, he could hear voices chattering happily. But there were way too many to make out what anyone was saying. Beneath the chatter, Tucker could hear the clink of glasses, dishes, and silverware being used.

Tucker looked around at his surroundings. In front of him was a low cabinet made of dark, intricately carved wood. Behind its glass doors, the cabinet held shelves of delicate teacups. Tucker glanced down at his hand. They were identical to the teacup he was still holding.

"I think we are on the boat," Tucker said. "We must be in the pantry or something."

"But we're not moving," Maya said. "We're not bobbing around on the ocean."

Tucker got to his feet. "We might be," he said. "The *Titanic* was — I mean is — enormous. It'd be hard to feel the waves on a ship that big."

"If you say so," Maya said. She started to stand too.

Tucker suddenly dropped back to his knees. "Stay down!" he hissed at Maya. He pulled her back to the ground.

"Hey, take it easy," she snapped. "What's your problem?"

"See for yourself," Tucker whispered. He motioned to the area above the cabinet.

Slowly, Maya raised herself up onto her knees so she could see over the cupboard. They weren't in some kind of storage room for dishes and cups, like they'd originally thought. They were in an enormous dining room. The room looked at least one hundred feet long. Floor-to-ceiling windows stretched the entire length of the far wall. Out the windows, there was nothing to see but ocean and sky for miles.

Around the room, there was enough seating for the hundreds of people. Most of the tables seemed full. Everyone was talking and laughing and enjoying their food. White-coated waiters carried trays loaded with food to the passengers. The heavy oak furniture gave the room a sophisticated feeling.

Maya spotted the exit. It was all the way on the opposite side of the room. She and Tucker would have to sneak past all the diners and staff to get out.

Maya dropped back behind the cupboard. "There must be like five hundred people out there!" she whispered.

Tucker nodded. "I don't know how we're going to get all the way across the room to the exit," he said. "We're trapped here. We should have brought the right clothes this time. I can't believe I didn't think of it."

Maya smiled. "I don't think it really matters," she said.

"Are you kidding?" he said. He gestured at their clothes. "We'll look like total weirdos if anyone sees us in these clothes. Everyone out there is dressed for 1912, not 2012."

"So?" Maya asked.

"So we'll get caught," Tucker said.

"And?" Maya said. "What are they going to do? Throw us in the ocean?"

"I guess not. . . ." Tucker said. "So what do you think we should do?"

Maya stood up. Tucker tried to grab her wrist, but she pulled it away. "You worry too much," she said. "Let's just find someone who works here and ask them where to find Liam."

"Ask someone?!" Tucker said loudly, jumping to his feet. "Are you crazy?!"

The room went silent. Tucker turned around. Everyone in the dining hall was staring at him and Maya.

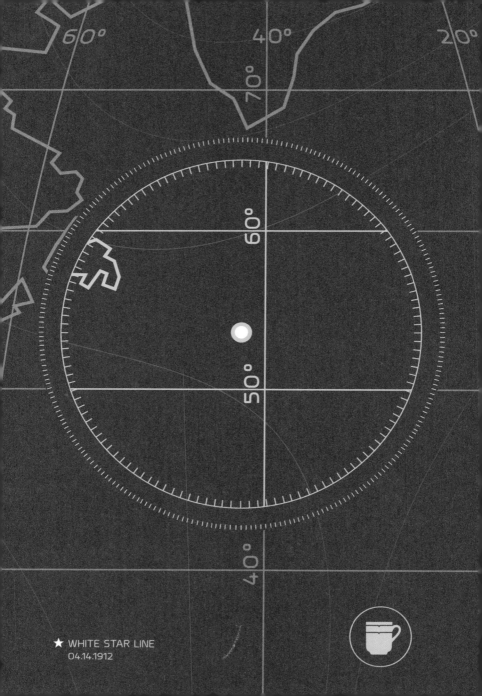

60°　40°　20°

70°

60°

50°

40°

★ WHITE STAR LINE
04.14.1912

## LOW CLASS

4

The diners muttered with disapproval. They clearly weren't used to having their meal disrupted.

Tucker quickly slipped the Special Collection teacup into Maya's hand. If they lost that, they also lost their way home. "Put this in your bag," he said quietly. She did.

A moment later, a man in a dark uniform appeared beside them. His uniform had shiny brass buttons and he wore a white hat with a narrow brim. He had a big bushy mustache and a very stern look on his face.

"What are you two doing in the galley?" he asked. "Come out here."

Maya and Tucker stepped out from behind the cabinet. The man's stern look got even sterner. "What on earth are you two wearing?" he asked.

Maya and Tucker started to answer, but the man just shook his head and put up his hands. "Please," he said. "Don't bother with excuses. This is the first-class dining saloon, and you're obviously not first-class passengers. You know you're not allowed to be in here. You'll have to leave immediately."

"Happily," Tucker said. He took Maya by the hand and pulled her along. "Let's go."

Maya pulled her hand away. "Sir," she said
to the man in uniform, "can you help us find our
friend? His name is Liam Kearney."

The man sneered at Maya. "I can't possibly
remember every passenger onboard," he said.
"But if he's a friend of yours, he's probably not a
first-class passenger either. Which means he isn't
in here." The man started to usher them out of the
dining room.

"Can you at least tell us what the date is?"
Maya asked.

"Why do you care what the date is?" Tucker
whispered.

"Because the *Titanic* sank on April
fourteenth," Maya whispered. "What if that's
today? I don't know about you, but I'd like a little
warning if we're on a sinking ship."

"The date?" the man repeated. "It's April
fourteenth, of course. Now, out!"

Tucker and Maya exchanged a look. If it was
April 14th, they didn't have much time.

"Come on," Tucker snapped. "Let's go." He grabbed Maya's hand and pulled her after him. This time she followed him through the dining room toward the exit.

# R.M.S. "TITANIC"
## APRIL 14, 1912

### FIRST-CLASS DINNER

HORS D'OEUVRE VARIES
OYSTERS
CONSOMME OLGA, CREAM OF BARLEY
SALMON, MOUSSELINE SAUCE, CUCUMBER

FILET MIGNONS LILI
SAUTÉ OF CHICKEN LYONNAISE
VEGETABLE MARROW FARCIE
LAMB, MINT SAUCE
ROAST DUCKLING, APPLE SAUCE
SIRLOIN OF BEEF, CHATEAU POTATOES

GREEN PEAS, CREAMED CARROTS
BOILED RICE
PARMENTER & BOILED NEW POTATOES

PUNCH ROMAINE

ROAST SQUAB & CRESS
COLD ASPARAGUS VINAIGRETTE
PATÉ DE FOIE GRAS
CELERY

WALDORF PUDDING
PEACHES IN CHARTREUSE JELLY
CHOCOLATE & VANILLA ECLAIRS
FRENCH ICE CREAM

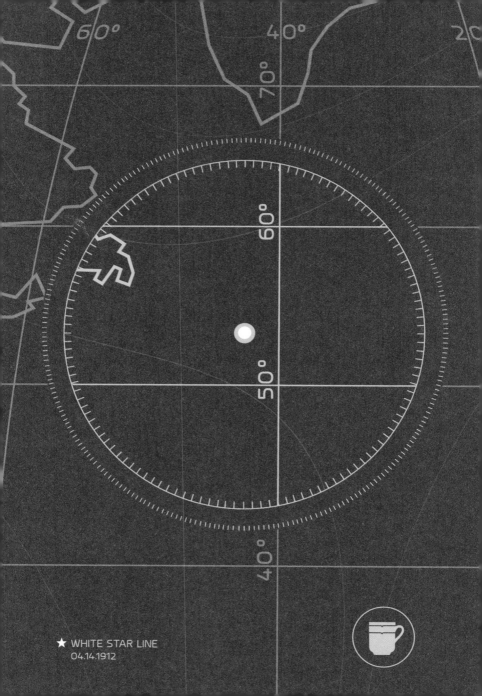

60°

40°

20

70°

60°

50°

40°

# TO THE POOL

Tucker and Maya exited the first-class dining room. They immediately found themselves in a smaller room that was just as fancy.

"This must be the first-class reception area," Maya whispered. The room was full of fancy wood furniture and gleaming chandeliers. The ceiling was painted bright white in sharp contrast to the rust-colored carpet. Everyone inside appeared to be first-class passengers. They were all outfitted in fancy, formal-looking clothing. Many were sitting at small tables, enjoying drinks before dinner.

"Everyone is staring at us," Tucker said. "I don't like this."

"Relax," Maya said. "They're just marveling at my amazing sense of fashion."

Tucker rolled his eyes. "Come on, let's get out of here," he said. Maya rolled her eyes but followed him out of the room.

"Where would a kid go on this ship?" Tucker asked. "We have to find the Kearneys right away."

Suddenly, the grand staircase appeared in front of them. It was amazing to see. Tucker and Maya stopped near the cherub statue at the base of the staircase and stared.

"Wow," Maya said. Her mouth dropped open. "It looks just like it did in the movie."

The grand staircase stretched up from where they stood. The staircase was sixteen feet wide with a central banister running up the middle. Twelve wide steps led to the top of the staircase, where a beautiful clock was surrounded by intricately carved wood. The staircase was framed on both sides by ornate wooden banisters and iron scrollwork. Oak paneling gleamed all around.

The ceiling, sixty feet above the foyer, was a massive glass dome decorated with wrought iron. Moonlight shining in from outside illuminated the landing below. At the center of the dome hung a gleaming chandelier.

"I can't believe how huge it is," Maya whispered. "It's amazing."

"I know," Tucker agreed. "Can you believe all of this will be at the bottom of the ocean soon?"

Maya shook her head. "We'd better find Liam before that happens," she said. "Look, that clock says it's already 8:00 p.m. *Titanic* hits the iceberg at 11:40 p.m. We have to find Liam and his family before then."

Tucker leaned down and set his watch to match the time on the clock. "That way we'll know how much time we have left to find the Kearneys," he explained when Maya gave him a weird look.

"Plus, we have to convince the captain to change course and figure out how to get ourselves

back to 2012," Maya added. "We don't have a lot of time. Let's go."

Maya walked over to one of the first-class passengers who'd just descended the grand stairway. The man, wearing in a fancy suit and holding a cigar in his mouth, stared down at them.

"Excuse me, sir," Maya said. "Can you help me and my friend?"

"Eh?" the man said. "What's that? I'm on my way to the smoking lounge. I don't have time for this. Who are you two? Should you even be on this deck?"

Maya ignored his question. "We're looking for our friend," she said.

"Well, if he's as odd as you two," the man said, "I'd remember him." He laughed.

"Where would a kid our age go on this ship?" Maya asked.

The man shrugged. "How should I know?" he muttered. He started to walk away. Halfway across the foyer he called back to Maya and

Tucker, "Try the pool, for goodness sake. But don't bother me any more."

Maya smiled. "Ah," she said. "The pool. I was hoping we'd visit the pool."

"Wait a minute," Tucker said. "How did you even know there was a pool?"

Maya shrugged. "I told you, I read a little online last night," she said. "I was curious. Plus I knew you'd want to try and come back. I figured at least one of us should be prepared."

Tucker looked impressed. "Good thinking," he said.

"I know," Maya said with a smirk. "Anyway, come on. It's this way. We have to get down to the F deck. We're on D . . . I think."

"This better not be a waste of time," Tucker said. But when Maya started off at a rapid pace, he followed her.

* * *

It was a long walk, down two flights of stairs, to find the pool. Tucker had no idea how Maya knew where to go. Or even where they were. He was almost positive they were lost. But soon, he found himself at a door marked "POOL" on a small sign.

Maya walked right up to the door and pulled it open. But before she could walk in, someone took her by the shoulders and steered her right back out. "Hold it, you," the man said. "Where do you think you're going, miss?"

Maya and Tucker stood side by side. The man blocking the door to the pool now was in a uniform similar to the one worn by the man at the dining hall. But this man seemed much younger — maybe not even twenty. He had a kind face and no mustache. Despite his words, he was smiling.

"Now, listen," he said, still with a smile. "I

know how much you'd love to take a swim in the pool, but it's closed to third-class passengers."

"What makes you think we're third-class passengers?" Maya snapped.

The young crewman looked at her a moment, then at Tucker. Tucker looked down at his clothes and Maya's. They were both in jeans, and Tucker's jeans had tears at the knees. The crewman raised his eyebrows.

"Oh," Tucker said. "Right."

Maya waved him off. "These are really cool jeans," she said. "They're from a top designer."

Tucker rolled his eyes. Then he looked at the crewman. "Sir, we're sorry to show up in these rags," he said. "Our luggage was misplaced."

Maya started to protest, but Tucker cut her off. "I think my friend's mother is in there," Tucker said. "Can we just go in quickly to look?"

The crewman stood up straighter and looked down at the two kids. Maya flashed her most adorable smile. The crewman laughed.

"All right, you two," he said. "Go ahead then. But I'll have my eye on you. Don't dally!"

Maya and Tucker thanked the crewman and darted into the pool. It was very crowded. Tucker stopped and looked around.

Several people were in the pool, but no one was swimming. They were standing around and talking. Some kids splashed a little. But the funniest thing was their bathing suits.

The men and women were covered from neck to ankle in heavy, dark-colored suits. Only their faces and arms were exposed. *Even if they want to swim,* Tucker thought, *they'd hardly be able to move in those outfits.*

Maya didn't seem to notice. She glanced over her shoulder to make sure she was hidden from the crewman's view. Then she opened her bag.

Tucker jogged to catch up to her. "What are you doing?" he asked. "We're supposed to be looking for Liam."

"You heard the crewman," Maya said.

"Third-class passengers aren't allowed in here. Liam's family is in third class. So he won't be in here."

"Then let's go someplace else to find him," Tucker said.

"No way!" Maya said. Then she did something that completely shocked Tucker: she kicked off her shoes and started unbuttoning her jeans.

"What are you doing?" Tucker shouted. He pushed Maya farther out of sight.

"Don't push me, Tucker," Maya snapped. "I'm going for a swim, obviously. I have my suit on under this."

"Wait a minute," Tucker said. "Why are you wearing a bathing suit under your clothes?"

"I told you," Maya said. She pulled a towel from her bag. "I read about the *Titanic* online last night, and I learned about the pool. So I planned ahead."

"I don't think that's a good idea," Tucker said.

"Why not? It's a pool, isn't it?" Maya said. She

pulled off her T-shirt. She was wearing a bright blue two-piece bathing suit with a funky, paisley pattern underneath.

"You're amazing," Tucker said, shaking his head.

"Thank you," Maya said.

"But I still don't think this is a good idea," Tucker said.

"Relax," Maya said. "We have hours. I'm just going to take a short swim. *Titanic* doesn't hit the iceberg until 11:40 pm. We'll still have plenty of time to find Liam."

"Do you know how big this ship is?" Tucker argued. "Let's go!"

"You're forgetting something important. We're supposed to be on vacation," Maya said. She started for the pool. "If I can't go to the beach like a normal person, I will use a pool. Now watch my perfect butterfly stroke."

Maya walked right to the edge of the pool. Tucker could hardly watch as she put her feet

together and dove into the pool with hardly a splash. Some people gasped. Tucker heard a man say, "My word!"

No one made a sound as Maya swam the length of the pool. When she came up for air, everyone in the pool was staring at Maya. Everyone in the deck chairs around the pool sat up straight. And everyone was completely silent.

"Um," Maya said, "is there a problem?"

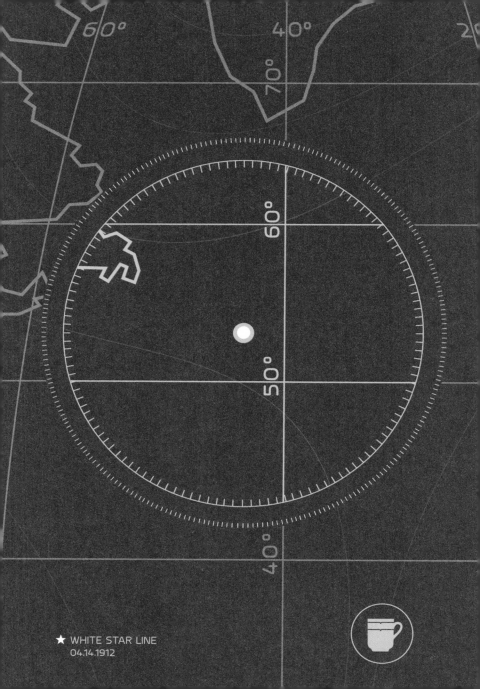

60° 40° 2°

70°

60°

50°

40°

★ WHITE STAR LINE
04.14.1912

# SQUASH

Tucker grabbed a towel and ran to the edge of
the pool to help Maya climb out.

"You can't wear that!" Tucker said in a loud,
angry whisper.

"What are you talking about?" Maya asked,
looking down at her bathing suit.

"Everyone is staring at you!" Tucker said.
"By 1912 standards, you might as well have run
through the dining hall in your underwear!"

Maya stood on the edge of the pool and
accepted the towel Tucker was holding out to her.
"I thought everyone was impressed with my dive,"
Maya said, "and my butterfly stroke."

"Doubtful," Tucker said. He put an arm around Maya and led her toward the door. He looked down at his watch. It was already 9:30. "Let's just get out of here."

"Hold it," a voice said. Maya and Tucker turned. The crewman who'd let them in was standing right behind them. "I think you two have some explaining to do."

"Um, the truth is, sir," Tucker said, "we're looking for a friend of ours. But he's not here."

The crewman looked at Maya, who was now shivering in her towel. "You'd better get dressed, lassie," he said. "You can use the changing rooms." He pointed at a door in the corner. "Be quick," he added as Maya grabbed her bag and hurried away.

The crewman turned back to Tucker. "So you weren't looking for her mother," he said.

Tucker shook his head.

The crewman took off his hat and sighed as he scratched his head. "You two could have gotten me in a lot of trouble," he said.

"I'm really sorry," Tucker said.

The crewman nodded and put his hat back on. "When your friend gets back, you two had better clear out," he said. "Head back to the third-class common room, or you're bound to get in serious trouble. Is that clear?"

"Yes, sir," Tucker said.

Maya walked up just then. She was back in her jeans and T-shirt. Her hair was still wet.

"Let's go," Tucker said. He took Maya by the wrist and pulled her toward the door.

"What happened?" Maya asked.

"Just hurry up," Tucker told her.

The crewman watched them leave, shaking his head.

"Where to now?" Maya asked once they were out of sight of the pool. Tucker was stomping through the narrow halls of Deck F.

"Are you mad at me or something?" Maya said, hurrying to keep up. She grabbed Tucker's shoulder and he stopped to face her.

"No," he snapped. "But I am trying to hurry and find Liam before this ship hits an iceberg and sinks. That's why we're here. Remember?"

"Yeah. I remember," Maya said quietly.

"Yeah, well, you don't seem to be taking this very seriously," Tucker said. "You're the one who pointed out that *Titanic* is going to hit an iceberg at 11:40. We don't have much time."

"So you are mad at me," Maya said.

"Fine, yes," Tucker said. "A little."

Maya looked down. "I want to find Liam too," she said. "I really thought he'd be at the pool. I mean, it's where I would go, if I were him."

"You heard that crewman. He's not allowed!" Tucker said.

Maya shrugged. "We weren't allowed either," she said. "But that didn't stop me from going swimming, did it?"

Tucker squinted at her. "No . . ." he said slowly.

"I guess I just figured, even in 1912, if Liam wanted to go swimming, he'd find a way," Maya said. "That's what I would have done, at least."

Tucker sighed. "I guess that makes sense," he said. "Listen, we only have a few hours until *Titanic* hits the iceberg. We need to focus on finding Liam."

"Okay, agreed," Maya said. "Do you want to hear my other idea?"

"Sure," Tucker said.

"Squash," Maya said.

"Squash?" Tucker said. "Like, a pumpkin or a zucchini or something?"

Maya giggled. "Not squash the food," she said. "Squash the sport!"

"Squash what sport?" Tucker said. "How do you squash a sport?"

"No, squash *is* a sport," Maya said. She started walking and gestured for Tucker to follow her. "It's a lot like racquetball. Actually, it might be the same thing. I'm not sure. Anyway, the court is over here."

Tucker followed Maya down another narrow hallway. He could hear the sound of a ball slapping against a wall and the sound of feet shuffling and squeaking across the floor.

Two men sat on a bench outside the door to one of the squash courts. They were laughing and smoking. One of them stood up when he saw Tucker and Maya approach.

For an instant, Tucker thought the man looked familiar, but he couldn't think of why.

*Where do I know him from?* Tucker thought. Then he realized. The man was Mr. Kearney.

Just then, Mr. Kearney met Tucker's gaze. Mr. Kearney's eyes narrowed in recognition.

"Uh-oh," Tucker muttered. He grabbed Maya by the arm. "We should go. Now."

"Hey!" Mr. Kearney shouted. His face went red with anger. "I know those two brats. Stop! Someone stop those two! They're stowaways!"

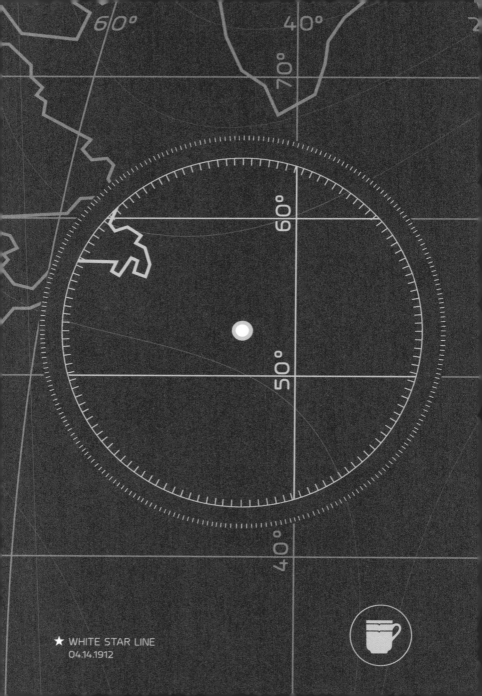

# 7

# STOWAWAYS!

Tucker turned and ran, still holding Maya's arm. Behind them, crewmen were blowing whistles and calling for officers. Someone shouted, "Two stowaways on Deck F!"

"What's going on?" Maya said. She ran too, struggling to keep up with Tucker.

"Don't you know who that was?" Tucker asked. He led her into a stairwell and up to Deck E.

"Who?" Maya asked. "What are you talking about?"

"That was Liam's father," Tucker said. "He remembers us from the dock and from the tender we took out to the *Titanic*."

"Oh, great," Maya said. "What does he have against us, anyway?"

Tucker turned a corner and the hall got even narrower. Soon they reached another set of steps. Tucker darted up them with Maya right on his heels.

"Who knows why he hates us?" Tucker said. "But he knows we shouldn't be onboard."

"Shouldn't we have asked him where Liam is, at least?" Maya said.

"He didn't really seem like he was in a helpful mood when he was calling security on us," Tucker pointed out. "Come on, we need to hide. I don't know what they did with stowaways in the old days, but I know I don't want to find out."

Tucker yanked open the door at the top of the

stairs. He and Maya emerged onto Deck C and started down another narrow hallway. There were dozens of doors now.

"These must be private rooms or something," Tucker said. "Maybe we can find an open door."

Maya nodded. They ran along the hall, trying door after door. But every door was locked.

They reached the end of the hallway and took a sharp turn at top speed. They ran right into a crewman.

He jumped back. "Whoa, you two," the man said. "Where's the fire?"

Tucker started to apologize. "Sorry, sir. We —" he began. Then he saw the young man's face. It was the crewman from the pool.

"Say, it's you two again," the crewman said. He smiled. "Where are you running off to now? Still looking for your friend?"

"That's right," Maya said. "I'm Maya, by the way. And this is Tucker."

The young crewman put out his hand for Tucker to shake. "A pleasure to make your acquaintance," he said. "I'm Seaman Terrell, but you may call me Bert. And I'm glad I've run into you again, if you'll pardon the pun."

"Why are you glad?" Tucker asked. He hoped their new friend hadn't been looking for them because they were stowaways.

"I believe I've found your friend," Bert said.

Tucker and Maya's eyes went wide. "You have?" they both said.

Bert nodded. "I've just been to the third-class common room," he said. He turned and pointed down the hallway to indicate the room. "I met a boy reading a Sexton Blake story. I happen to enjoy Sexton Blake myself, so we started talking."

"Who?" Maya asked. She glanced at Tucker to see if he knew what Bert was talking about. But Tucker just shrugged.

"Why, the great detective, Sexton Blake," Bert said. He took off his cap and scratched his head. "Don't they have him in America? I suppose not."

Tucker shrugged again.

"In any event," Bert went on, "the boy I spoke to was looking for two very unusual American children. I immediately thought of you two."

"Thanks . . ." Maya said. "I think."

Tucker beamed. "Thank you so much," he said. "Thank you!"

Bert smiled at them and pulled out his pocket watch to check the time. "Well, I'd best be getting back to work now," he said.

As Bert tucked his watch back into the pocket of his uniform, Tucker caught a glimpse of the watch's face: ten o'clock.

Tucker turned to Maya. "Come on," he said. "Let's go,"

Tucker and Maya ran off toward the common room. "Slow down!" Bert called from behind them. His laughter followed them down the narrow hall.

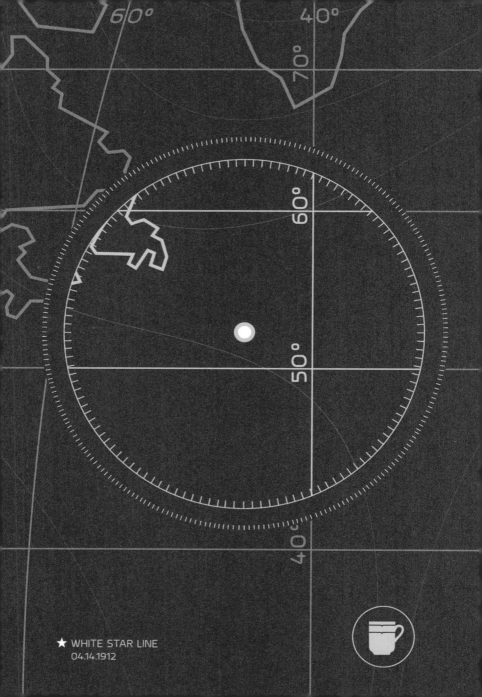

THE **COMMON ROOM**

8

Tucker and Maya stepped into the third-class common room. It was a loud, noisy place. Against the far wall, someone was playing a piano. In the center of the room, a big group of adults was singing and dancing. The place was full of smoke, and it smelled strongly of body odor.

Maya covered her nose. "Oh, gross. Don't these people shower?" she said over the din.

Tucker shook his head. "I guess not," he said. Across the room, Tucker spotted a boy sitting by himself with a book open in his lap.

"There he is!" Tucker said. He and Maya pushed through the room and stopped in front of the bench.

"Hello, Liam," Tucker said.

The boy looked up. When he saw Tucker and Maya, he beamed. "Boy, am I glad to see you two," he said.

"We've been looking everywhere for you," Tucker said.

"And having zero fun," Maya added, glaring at Tucker.

"We've been kicked out of the pool and squash courts," Tucker said, "and we just got chased all over the ship by half the crew. Your father reported us as stowaways!"

"Sounds terribly exciting!" Liam said. "What fun!"

"What're you reading?" Tucker asked, changing the subject.

Liam handed him the book.

"Oh, Sexton Blake," Tucker said, looking at the cover. He flipped through the pages. "Bert mentioned this. Looks pretty cool."

"Cool?" Liam repeated. He looked confused.

No. 123.—"THE BOYS' FRIEND" 3d. LIBRARY.

SEXTON BLAKE IN THE CONGO!
A TALE OF THRILLING ADVENTURE
IN RUBBER LAND.

3D.

MAGNIFICENT LONG, COMPLETE TALE OF ADVENTURE

"Um, that is," Tucker said, "it looks good. I think I'd like it."

"You don't know Sexton Blake?" Liam asked. He took the book back. "You two sure are odd."

"Can we get back on track?" Maya said. "We've been looking for Liam, and it wasn't to have a geeky talk about books or something."

"Yes. We have to convince the captain to change course," Tucker said. "Maybe if we head south, it will be safer."

Liam shook his head. "It won't work," he said. "I've spoken to half the crew about it. Even Bert won't listen. At least he's nice about it. Everyone else thinks I'm just a silly child playing a game."

"Well, I refuse to give up," Tucker said. "Maya, do you think you can find the captain's quarters?"

Liam's eyes went wide. "You can't just walk into the captain's quarters!" he said.

"Why not?" Maya asked.

"It's not allowed," Liam said. "You're third-class children."

The piano playing and singing suddenly stopped. Tucker turned. A group of crewmen stood at the entrance to the common room. And they didn't look happy.

"Worse than that," Tucker said. "We're stowaways."

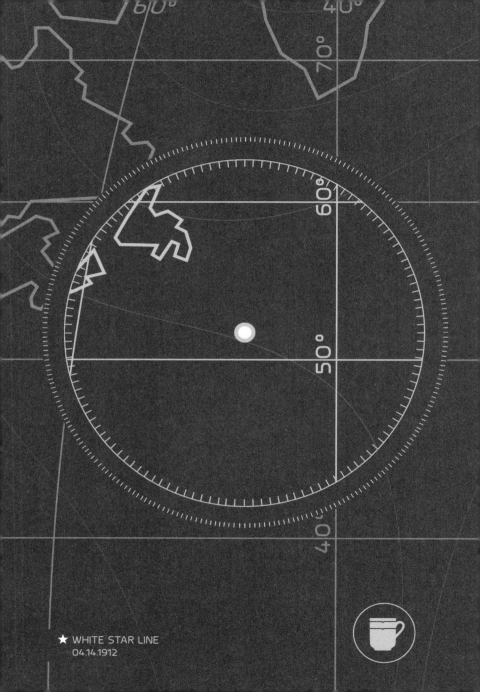

★ WHITE STAR LINE
04.14.1912

## CHASED

Just then, one of the crewmen caught sight of Maya and Tucker. He pointed across the room. "There they are!" he shouted. "Don't move, you two!"

"Run!" Tucker hollered.

Tucker and Maya darted around the common room. Crewmen dove and grabbed at them. But the third-class passengers enjoyed every moment. Instead of grabbing the kids and turning them in, the passengers laughed and hollered, sometimes even tripping a crewman or helping Maya and Tucker to hide for a moment.

Liam ran for the door. "This way!" he called to Maya and Tucker.

Maya and Tucker were on opposite sides of the big common room, dodging crewmen, hiding under tables, and ducking behind benches and couches. They ran toward the center of the room, toward each other. Each had a crewman right behind them. Just as they were about to collide, Maya turned right and Tucker turned left. They ran for the door, where Liam was frantically waving for them.

The two crewmen ran right into each other.

"Well done!" Liam shouted. "Now follow me!"

Liam led the two Americans to a stairwell. The three friends climbed the narrow metal steps. When Liam threw open the door on the boat deck, a frigid wind nearly blew them down.

"The bridge is up this way!" Liam shouted against the wind.

Maya and Tucker followed their Irish friend as he scurried across the deck. They reached the door of the bridge. Tucker banged and banged until it flew open.

"What's this, then?" the captain asked. He stood in the open doorway and glared down at them.

The captain wore a white uniform and had a white beard. He could have been one of their grandfathers. To Tucker, he looked a little like Santa Claus, if Santa Claus was very, very angry because he had been woken up.

"Captain Smith?" Liam said.

The captain looked down at the boy. His face went red. He balled his hands into fists. "Yes?" he said.

"Um," Liam said, "these American children have something to tell you." He stepped to the side.

Tucker tried to smile, but the captain's anger made him very nervous. "Sir," Tucker said, "we were wondering if you'd be willing to change course. Just a little bit?"

Maya and Liam nodded vigorously.

"Turn the boat?" Captain Smith asked. He shook his head, as if he couldn't believe what he was seeing. Then he looked over the children's heads. A group of crewmen were approaching.

"Please take these children back to wherever they belong," Captain Smith told the crewmen. "Besides," he added quickly, glancing at Tucker, "the ship's course has already been altered slightly. To the south."

"It has?" Tucker said. "Why?"

"We've received multiple iceberg warnings," he said. "We're moving south to avoid an ice field."

Tucker heard Maya breathe a sigh of relief next to him. If the captain already knew about the iceberg warnings then the problem was solved. They'd managed to prevent a disaster.

Just then, Tucker felt a firm hand on his shoulder. "These two are stowaways," a crewman said. "What shall we do with them?"

"Hmm," the captain said. "We've no brig on this ship."

"They can stay with the stewardesses, Captain," a voice said.

Maya and Tucker turned to see who'd spoken. It was Bert. He winked at them.

"I'll make sure they stay out of trouble," Bert added.

The captain grunted. "Fine, fine," he said. "When we reach New York, we'll hand them over to the proper authorities. And the Irish lad?"

"His parents are in third class, sir," Bert said. "I'll make sure he's confined to quarters."

"Very good," the captain said. "Now, I'll not be disturbed again tonight." Then he stepped back into his room and shut the door.

The crewmen dispersed, except Bert.

"I knew you three would end up causing trouble," he said, smiling at Maya, Tucker, and Liam.

"Sorry," Tucker said. "We didn't mean to upset anyone. I guess the captain knew about the icebergs after all."

Bert nodded. "Of course he did," he said. "He's one of the finest captains in the world."

He led the three kids below to the lower decks.

"Liam, I'll drop you off at your parents' quarters," Bert said. "Then, Maya and Tucker, I'll leave you with Miss Jessop. She's one of the stewardesses and a friend of mine. She'll keep you out of trouble and make sure you get fed."

Bert led them down several flights of stairs and a long hallway. At Liam's room, the three children exchanged a long look. They knew they might never see each other again. But Maya and Tucker were happy. At least Liam and his family were safe.

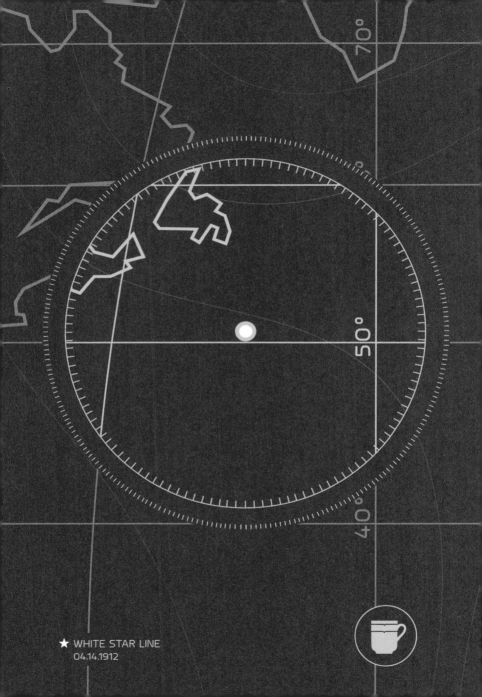

★ WHITE STAR LINE
04.14.1912

OUT OF TIME

Violet Jessop yawned as she opened the door to her quarters. She wore an old-fashioned nightgown and looked confused. It was clear that she'd already been sleeping when Bert knocked on her door.

"Seaman Terrell?" she said. "Who are these children?"

"Two American stowaways," Bert replied. "Meet Maya and Tucker. I told the captain I'd keep them out of trouble."

"So they've become my trouble, have they?" Violet asked, but she smiled as she said it.

"I've got to get back to duty or people will be wondering where I've gone," Bert said. "I'm on overnight. Good evening, Miss Jessop."

Bert tipped his hat to the stewardess.

Then he patted Maya on the head. "I'll see you two in the morning," he said. He smiled at them before turning and walking off down the long hallway.

"That's what he thinks," Maya whispered to Tucker. "I don't know about you, but as soon as Miss Jessop goes back to sleep I'm going back to the present."

Tucker smiled. He couldn't believe it, but they'd finally managed to accomplish what they'd come back to do. The captain had altered the ship's course. *Titanic* would miss the iceberg. Now that the Kearneys were safe there was no reason to stay. Maya was right. It was time to get back to their own lives.

Violet put her hands on her hips. "All right, Maya and Tucker," she said. "It's very late, and I'm very tired. I've had a long day dealing with passengers, and tomorrow is sure to be more of the same. You two will have to sleep on the floor, I'm afraid."

"That's all right," Maya said. She shot Tucker a knowing look. "Don't worry about us. I have a feeling neither or us will be getting much sleep tonight anyway."

Violet nodded sympathetically. "Too excited, I expect," she said. "That's understandable. I still get excited by ocean voyages as well, and I've been on quite a few."

She led them inside. Violet shared the quarters with several other stewardesses. The room was small and cramped. Small beds lined the walls. Maya and Tucker could see that the other stewardesses were already asleep.

Violet pulled a couple of small pillows and thin blankets out of a cupboard. She set them down on the floor for Maya and Tucker.

She let out a wide yawn. "We can get better acquainted in the morning," she said. Within moments, Violet was back in her little bed and snoring gently.

"Okay, let's go," Maya whispered. She started to sit up.

"Let's wait to make sure she's really asleep. Then we can sneak out and go find Liam," Tucker whispered. "We should at least say goodbye before we go back to the present."

"Why do you care so much?" Maya whispered back. She lay back down on the floor and stared into the dark.

Tucker thought about it. "I don't know," he admitted. "I feel a connection to Liam." He slowly got to his feet and crept to the door. None of the stewardesses stirred. "Are you going to come with me or not?" he asked. He pushed open the cabin door. The hallway was nearly as dark as the cabin.

Maya sighed, but she stood up. "Fine," she whispered. "Wait for me."

She hurried out into the hallway and pulled the door silently closed. "Do you even know where you're going?" Maya asked.

"I think so," Tucker replied. "It's tough to be sure in the dark, but I think we're pretty close to where Bert dropped off Liam."

He and Maya moved slowly down a hallway of third-class quarters. Tucker stopped at a door. "I think this is it," he whispered.

Maya lifted her fist to knock. But as her hand touched the wooden door, a deafening screech and boom rang through the ship. The floor shook under their feet.

Alarm bells sounded. Maya and Tucker stumbled against the wall. Maya fell to the floor, and her bag flew from her shoulder.

"The teacup!" she shouted, but it was too late. The cup went flying from the open tote bag. It crashed against the floor and shattered.

NEW YORK

GREENVILLE

# FAILED AGAIN

Tucker's head pounded. "Ugh," he moaned. "I feel like I was hit by a bus."

Maya sat up next to him. "Close," she said. "I think it was an iceberg."

Tucker sat up and shook his head. He looked around. He and Maya were sitting next to each other beside the Special Collection box, back in the museum storeroom.

"We failed," Tucker said. "Again."

Maya nodded. "Yep," she said. "That ship is sunk." She got up and dug through the crate.

"The teacup is okay," she said, pulling it out of the box. The teacup was back in its case, totally unharmed.

Just then, the storeroom door opened. Mrs. Paulsen stood in the doorway. When she saw Maya standing there, holding the teacup, her mouth fell open.

"Maya!" Mrs. Paulsen said. She hurried over and grabbed the teacup. "Please tell me you weren't about to open this case."

"Of course not, Mrs. Paulsen," Maya said innocently. "Especially not after yesterday."

But Mrs. Paulsen spotted the broken remains of a plastic case—the one from the teacup they'd used to travel. Tucker spotted it at the same time.

"How could that —," he started to say.

"What is this?!" Mrs. Paulsen said. She stomped over and picked up a piece of the plastic case. "And broken! Tucker, can you explain this? Where is the cup that was in this case?"

"It's not what you think," Tucker said. He jumped to his feet. "That teacup . . . I mean, it's fine. It's right there!" He pointed at the one Maya was holding.

"That teacup is still in its case," his mom said. She looked really angry. "Tucker, I'm very disappointed in you. Lying to me, breaking rules. This is so unlike you."

Mrs. Paulsen turned to Maya. "And Maya," she said, "please don't make me regret letting you visit with us at the museum for your vacation."

Maya and Tucker looked at their feet.

Mrs. Paulsen sighed and ran her hands through her hair. "This is your second and final warning," she said a little more calmly. "Tomorrow, there will be none of this assistant curator stuff."

"What?!" Tucker said. He knew that meant they wouldn't be able to get to the Special Collection — and back to the ship to help Liam and his family.

Mrs. Paulsen shook her head. "Don't act so surprised," she said. "After this behavior, what did you expect me to do? Starting right now, you two will remain in the staff conference room, where you will do your homework."

"I don't have any homework for vacation," Maya said quietly.

Mrs. Paulsen turned to leave. "Then you can study or read," she said. "You can use your laptop. But that's all. And no comics for you, Tucker!"

She held the door open and waited for Tucker and Maya to follow her out. When neither of them made a move to leave, she stared at them expectantly and pointed out the open door to the hallway.

With their heads down, the kids left the storeroom and headed toward the conference room.

They sat down at the big wooden table in the center of the room. Mrs. Paulsen put a couple of books from the museum's library in front of them. "Tomorrow, you will bring your school books," she said. "For today, these will do. Enjoy."

Then she left them alone to work.

"This stinks," Tucker muttered under his breath.

"Yeah, no kidding," Maya said. "So much for vacation."

"And so much for helping Liam and his family," Tucker said. But he knew that somehow, he and Maya would find a way to try again . . . tomorrow.

# RETURN TO TITANIC

CONTINUES IN BOOK

1 2 3 4 •

**AN UNSINKABLE SHIP**

RETURN TO TITANIC

TIME VOYAGE

by STEVE BREZENOFF

1

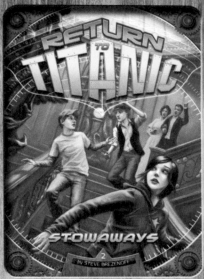

RETURN TO TITANIC

STOWAWAYS

by STEVE BREZENOFF

2

RETURN TO TITANIC

AN UNSINKABLE SHIP

by STEVE BREZENOFF

3

RETURN TO TITANIC

OVERBOARD

by STEVE BREZENOFF

4

# PASSENGER MANIFEST

While Tucker, Maya, and Liam are all fictional characters, the story of the *RMS Titanic* and its passengers is very real. In fact, some characters throughout the "Return to Titanic" series are based on real people.

| 1 |  | **JOHN COFFEY** FIREMAN |
| 2 |  | **VIOLET JESSOP** STEWARDESS |
| 3 |  | **JOHN JACOB ASTOR IV** FIRST-CLASS PASSENGER |
| 4 | | **EDWARD SMITH** CAPTAIN |

# *Violet Jessop*

## VIOLET JESSOP

Violet Jessop, a character featured in *Stowaways*, was a real stewardess aboard the *Titanic* when it set sail on its maiden voyage in April 1912. Born in 1887 in Buenos Aires, Argentina, Violet began her sea career when she was just 21 years old aboard the *RMS Orinoco*. She would go on to spend 42 years of her life at sea as a nurse and stewardess.

Violet's job as a stewardess aboard the *Titanic* earned her three pounds a month. Amazingly, before setting sail on *Titanic*, Violet had survived the near sinking of the *RMS Olympic* in 1911. She would go on to survive the sinking of the *HMHS Britannic* in 1916. Both the *Olympic* and the *Britannic* were sister ships to the *Titanic*.

Despite these close calls, Violet never gave up. She took her final assignment at sea at the age of 61. When Violet passed away from heart failure in 1971, she was 84 years old.

# HISTORICAL FILES

When *Titanic* set sail in April 1912, the separation between social classes was very obvious. The more than 2,200 passengers aboard the luxury ocean liner were segregated into first, second, and third class.

First-Class Teacup
circa 1912

First-class passengers aboard the *Titanic* had some of the best, most luxurious accommodations of the times. They had access to a gym, squash courts, a swimming pool, Turkish baths, and much more. Not surprisingly, first-class tickets were the most expensive. A first-class parlor suite cost $2,500, which would be about $57,200 today. The most expensive rooms would cost more than $103,000 in today's currency.

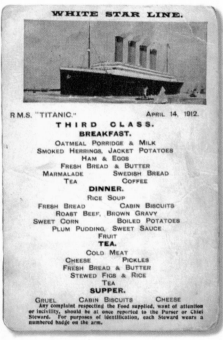

Third-Class Menu
April 14, 1912

While some could afford the more elegant first-class accommodations, the majority of passengers aboard the *Titanic* were in third class. Many of them were moving to America in the hopes of starting new lives. While third-class rooms were not nearly as grand as first-class areas, they were impressive compared to other third-class lodging at the time. Third-class cabins, which housed up to ten people, had electric lighting, heat, and wash basins. Third-class passengers also had access to an open-air gathering area. A third-class ticket aboard the *Titanic* cost $40, around $900 today.

Sadly, the separation between classes also played a major role when it came to odds of survival. 60 percent of first-class passengers survived, but the odds of survival decreased from there. Only 44 percent of second-class passengers lived, while a mere 25 percent of third-class passengers survived the sinking.

## AUTHOR

Steve Brezenoff lives in St. Paul, Minnesota, with his wife, Beth, their son, Sam, and their small, smelly dog, Harry. Besides writing books, he enjoys playing video games, riding his bicycle, and helping middle-school students to improve their writing skills. Steve's ideas almost always come to him in his dreams, so he does his best writing in his pajamas.

## ILLUSTRATOR

At a young age, Scott Murphy filled countless sketchbooks with video game and comic book characters. After being convinced by his high school art teacher that he could make a living creating what he loves, Scott jumped headfirst into the artistic pool and hasn't come up for air since. He currently resides in New York City and loves every minute of it.

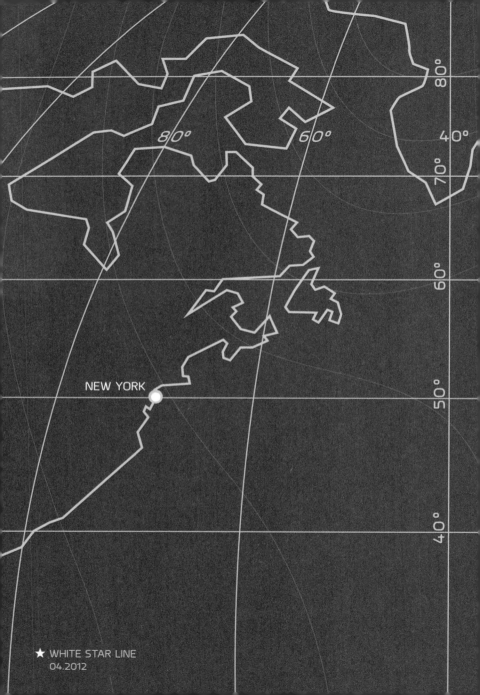

# RETURN TO TITANIC